THE BOY WHO
FOOLED THE GIANT

WHY THIS IS AN EASY READER

- This story has been carefully written to keep the young reader's interest high.

- It is told in a simple, open style, with a strong rhythm that adds enjoyment both to reading aloud and silent reading.

- There is a very high percentage of words repeated. It is this skillful repetition which helps the child to read independently. Seeing words again and again, he "practices" the vocabulary he knows, and learns with ease the words that are new.

- Only 208 different words have been used, with plurals and root words counted once.

   More than one-half of the words in this story have been used at least three times.

   Over one-fourth of the words in this story have been used at least six times.

   Some words have been used 37, 41 and 49 times.

ABOUT THIS STORY

- Folk tales like this one are part of the human past, and children find them deeply satisfying. This story is retold with imagination and humor, and genuine feeling for the folk-tale flavor.

- It lends itself happily to dramatization or part-playing, as well as expressive oral reading.

THE BOY WHO FOOLED THE GIANT

Story by TAMARA KITT
Pictures by WILLIAM RUSSELL
Editorial Consultant: LILIAN MOORE

GROSSET & DUNLAP • NEW YORK

By special arrangement with Wonder Books

Introduction

These books are meant to help the young reader discover what a delightful experience reading can be. The stories are such fun that they urge the child to try his new reading skills. They are so easy to read that they will encourage and strengthen him as a reader.

The adult will notice that the sentences aren't too long, the words aren't too hard, and the skillful repetition is like a helping hand. What the child will feel is: "This is a good story—and I can read it myself!"

For some children, the best way to meet these stories may be to hear them read aloud at first. Others, who are better prepared to read on their own, may need a little help in the beginning—help that is best given freely. Youngsters who have more experience in reading alone—whether in first or second or third grade—will have the immediate joy of reading "all by myself."

These books have been planned to help all young readers grow—in their pleasure in books and in their power to read them.

Lilian Moore
Specialist in Reading
Formerly of Division of Instructional Research,
New York City Board of Education

Far away and long ago

there was a boy.

He was nine years old.

But he was little.

He was so little,

everyone called him Little Billy.

His mother and his father

did not let him do anything.

They said he was too little.

Billy's father had a horse.

Did Billy's mother let him ride it?

Oh, no!

"You are too little," she said.

"I do not want you to get hurt."

Billy's father had a bow and arrow.

Did Billy's father let him use it?

Oh, no!

"You are too little," he said.

"I do not want you to get hurt."

"Maybe I am little," Billy said.

"But I can do big things.

Some day I will show them."

Now, not far away
there lived a giant.
The giant was very big.
He ate 100 cows for supper
every day.
And he ate 100 eggs for breakfast
every day.

He was eating all the cows.

He was eating all the eggs.

And he was drinking

all the water in all the rivers.

He was a mean giant, too.

Sometimes he jumped on houses—

SMASH!

It was fun for the giant.

But it was not fun

for anyone else.

He was a magic giant, too.
He could turn into anything
that he wanted to be.
He could turn into a tiger.

He could turn into a wild elephant.

He could turn into a dragon.

Everyone was afraid of the giant.

The King of the land said,

"Soon there will be nothing

to eat or drink.

Who will help us get rid

of this giant?

I will give lots of money

to the one who can get rid

of the giant."

So the King made a sign.

This is what it said:

18

See what I
will give to
the one who
can get rid
of the **giant**.

yours truly,
the **King**

Billy saw the King's sign.

"Maybe I am little," Billy said,

"but I can do big things.

Now I will show them."

19

So Billy made a sign.

This is what it said:

I am Billy

look out for me!

I'm the strongest boy

On land

or sea

Then Billy took a bag.

He put in a big white cheese.

The cheese looked like

a hard white stone.

He put in a stone, too.

21

He put in a little brown bird.

The bird looked like

a little brown ball.

He put in a little brown ball, too.

And he put in a big fly swatter.

Then Billy wrote a letter
to his mother and father.

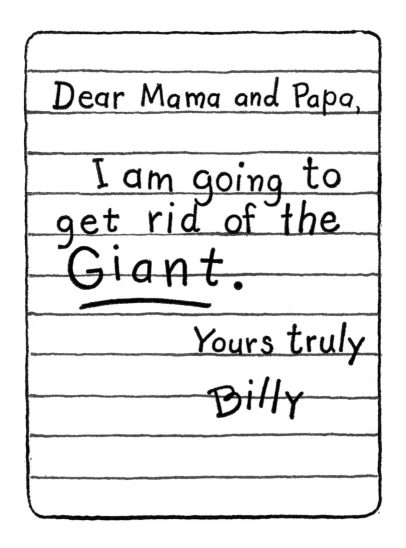

Dear Mama and Papa,

I am going to
get rid of the
Giant.

Yours truly
Billy

Billy took his bag.

And he took his sign.

And he began to walk.

He walked and walked.

He walked up a big hill.

And there was the giant's house.

Billy knocked.

Knock-knock.

No one came to the door.

Billy knocked again.

Knock-knock-knock.

No one came.

So Billy turned to go.

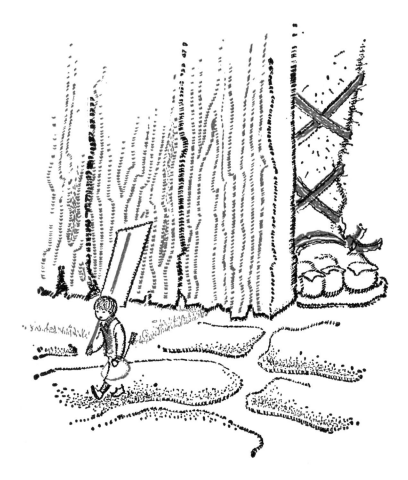

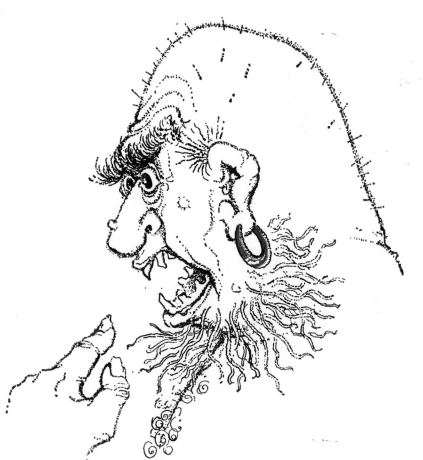

And there was the giant!

"Are you looking for ME?"

said the giant.

"Yes," Billy said.

"I'm looking for you."

"Aha! And who are YOU?"
said the giant.

"Look at my sign," said Billy.

The giant looked at the sign.

Then he began to laugh.

"Ha, ha, ha, ha!

Ho, ho, ho, ho!

Hee, hee, hee, hee!"

"So! YOU are the strongest boy
on land or sea?" said the giant.
And he began to laugh again.
"Ha, ha, ha, ha!
Ho, ho, ho, ho!
Hee, hee, hee, hee!"

"You can laugh all you want,"

Billy said.

"But I am stronger than you are.

I will show you."

"Well," said the giant,

"I have lots of gold in my house.

If you can show me you are stronger,

I will give you all the gold."

"I do not want your gold,"
Billy said.

"Aha!" said the giant.

"You are afraid!"

"No," Billy said.

"I am stronger than you are.

But I do not want your gold.

I will tell you what I want."

"Then tell me," said the giant.

"I want you to go far, far away,"
Billy said.

"You are eating all the cows.
You are eating all the eggs.
You are drinking all the water.
If I show you that I am stronger,
then you must go away."

"Very well," said the giant.

"First show me that
you are stronger."

"Well, then, take this stone,"
Billy said.

The giant took the stone.

"Now I will take a stone,"
Billy said.

And he took the white cheese
out of the bag.

"Now see me squeeze water
out of my stone," Billy said.
And he squeezed the cheese.
Water came out of it.
"Now YOU squeeze water
out of YOUR stone," Billy said.

The giant squeezed the stone.

Nothing came out.

The giant squeezed again.

He squeezed and squeezed.

But no water came out.

The giant was not laughing now.

"Look," Billy said.

"I will show you again

how strong I am.

I am so strong that I can throw

a ball higher than you can.

I can throw a ball so high,

it will not come down again."

42

"So can I," said the giant.

"Show me," said Billy.

Billy took the little brown ball

out of his bag.

He gave it to the giant.

"Now I will take this ball,"

Billy said.

He took the little brown bird

out of the bag.

"You go first,"

Billy said.

The giant's ball went up, up, up.

It looked like a little dot

in the sky.

The ball went so high that

they had to wait a long time

for it to come down.

"Now I will throw my ball,"
Billy said. And he did.
The little brown bird
went up, up, up.
It went higher and higher.
It looked like a little dot in the sky.
Then Billy and the giant
did not see it at all.

45

"My ball went so high," Billy said,
"that it will not come down."

"We will see about that,"
said the giant.

So they waited.

They waited and waited.

They waited a long, long time.

Nothing came down.

"You see?" Billy said.

"I am stronger than you!

I can squeeze water out of a stone.

And you can not. I can throw

a ball higher than you can.

So now you must go away."

"NO! NO! NO!" said the giant.

"I am stronger than you.

I am a magic giant.

I can turn

into a tiger.

See?"

"And I can turn
into a wild elephant.
See?"

"And I can turn
into a dragon.
See?"

"Yes. I see," Billy said.

"Well, then," said the giant,

"I will stay here as long as I want.

I will eat all the cows I want.

I will drink all the water I want.

And I will turn into a BIG tiger

and eat you, too."

Then Billy said,

"Your magic is strong magic.

But it is easy for a BIG giant

to turn into a BIG tiger.

Can you turn into a little cat?"

"Yes," said the giant.

"Show me," said Billy.

So the giant turned into a little cat.

Billy gave the cat a pat.

Then Billy said,

"That was pretty good.

But can you turn

into something VERY little?

Can you turn

into a very little mouse?"

"Yes!" said the giant.

"Show me," said Billy.

So the giant turned
into a very little mouse.
Billy gave the mouse some cheese.

"That was pretty good," Billy said.
"But there is one thing
you can not do."

"What?" said the giant.

"I can do anything."

"No," Billy said.

"You can not turn

into a very, very little fly.

That is too hard for you to do."

"Yes, I can," said the giant.

"Show me," said Billy.

So the giant turned into a fly
and —

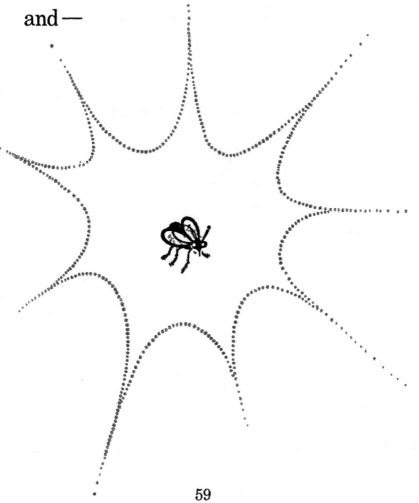

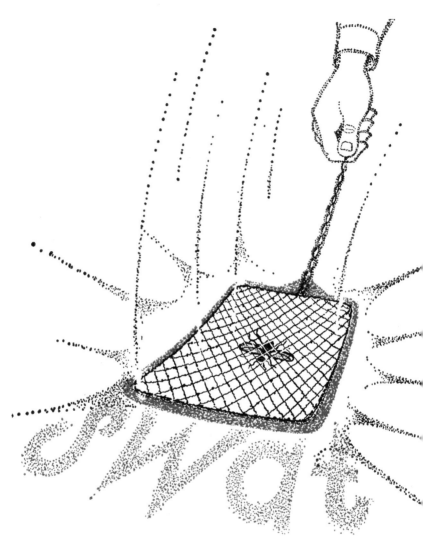

Billy killed the fly

with his fly swatter.

And that was the end of the giant.

CHOOSE FROM THESE EASY READERS

5901 Will You Come to My Party?
5902 Hurry Up, Slowpoke
5903 Mr. Pine's Mixed-up Signs
5904 The Adventures of Silly Billy
5905 The Secret Cat
5906 Billy Brown Makes Something Grand
5907 Miss Polly's Animal School
5908 The Duck on the Truck
5909 A Train for Tommy
5910 Surprise in the Tree
5911 The Monkey in the Rocket
5912 Billy Brown: The Baby Sitter
5913 Fly-Away at the Air Show
5914 Arty the Smarty
5915 The Surprising Pets of Billy Brown
5916 Barney Beagle
5917 I Made a Line
5918 Laurie and the Yellow Curtains
5919 Grandpa's Wonderful Glass
5920 Benjamin in the Woods
5921 Barney Beagle Plays Baseball
5922 The Day Joe Went to the Supermarket
5923 Question and Answer Book
5924 Let Papa Sleep!
5925 Jokes and Riddles
5926 The Surprise in the Story Book
5927 The Big Green Thing
5928 The Boy Who Fooled the Giant
5929 More Jokes and Riddles
5930 Too Many Pockets
5931 The Clumsy Cowboy
5932 Cat in the Box

THE BOY WHO
FOOLED THE GIANT